Penny

and the

PLAIN PIECE of PAPER

Miri Leshem-Pelly

PHILOMEL BOOKS

PHILOMEL BOOKS
An imprint of Penguin Random House LLC, New York

First published in the United States of America by Philomel,
an imprint of Penguin Random House LLC, 2020.

Visit us online at penguinrandomhouse.com

Library of Congress Cataloging-in-Publication Data is available
Manufactured in China
ISBN 9781984812728
10 9 8 7 6 5 4 3 2 1

Edited by Talia Benamy.
Design by Jennifer Chung.
Text set in Zemestro Book.

To Moti, with love

PENNY lived on a plain piece of paper.

"There's nothing here," she sighed. "I'm so bored. I wish I could live on a more interesting piece of paper."

So she decided to do something about it. She walked off her plain piece of paper and onto a . . .

BIG DEAL NEWS

Special Edition   ***   Weekend News   ***   Volume 2867

A NEW RULE

In a special government meeting, the new rule was addressed and registered as federal law. Some of the participants objected to the change and said that this was not the best decision. Law, who overlooked the meeting, was very happy with the final decision. "A new era is coming, all thanks to people who understand it. I thank all the participants of the meeting who understood the importance of this new rule and helped make it a reality."

Today will be the first meeting

of the committee that was assigned to work on applying the new rule, and within three weeks, all businesses across the country will begin to make the necessary changes in order to implement the rule.

"I'm looking forward to this new rule," said Mr. Order. "It will create growth in the economy and will make life a lot easier, especially for small business owners."

Continue reading on p. 3

NEWSPAPER

Penny walked along endless rows of small letters that told interesting stories.

Next to one of the stories, she found a picture of a man. "Who are you?" she asked him.

"I'm Mr. Important," he replied.

MR. IMPORTANT WILL SPEAK AT THE CONVENTION

The famous *Mr. Important* arrived this morning in the big city to participate in the big business convention. Mr. Busy, the head of the convention's committee, said, "We are thrilled to have such an honorable guest at our convention. I'm sure many participants will benefit a lot from listening to Mr. Important's speech. He is one of the most respected speakers in the world and always has many serious topics to talk about."

BUSINESS & ECONOMY NEWS

A new company named Big Trade has reported huge economic growth in the past three months, and their stocks rose by hundreds of percentage points.

We asked the company's manager, Ms. Success, to share the secret of this unusual growth. "We work very hard and we constantly listen to the market's needs," she replied. We also asked for

say that I love rules, and I think that rules are most important to our society. The new rule must be studied carefully and applied immediately in order for our economy to grow at a steady pace."

But not everybody shares the enthusiasm. "I think that Big Trade is about to go down fast," said an anonymous source. "When you go up so quickly,

SPORTS NEWS

A new world record was set yesterday at the big athletic competition. Mr. Fast made a significant achievement when he ran the race at the highest speed ever recorded in human history. He won the gold medal and said, "This is a great moment for me, and I'm sure this is just

BIG DEAL NEWS

Special Edition   ***   Weekend News   ***   Volume 2867

A NEW RULE

In a special government meeting, the new rule was accepted and registered as federal law. Some of the participants objected to the change and said that this would be a big mistake. Ms. L___ who offered the new rule, was ___ ___ with the decision and said, "A new era has now begun for many people who suffered until today. I thank all the participants of the meeting who understood the importance of this new rule and helped me to make it a reality."

Tomorrow will be the first meeting

of the committee that was assigned to work on applying the new rule, and within three ___, all businesses across the ___ will begin to make the new ___ ___ order to imple-

___ ___ ___ to this new rule," ___ ___ It will create growth in the ___ and will make life a lot easier ___ for small business owners."

Continue reading ...

> "Can I pose for a picture too?" Penny asked.
>
> "If you want to pose for a newspaper picture," said Mr. Important, "you should stand straight, hold your head up high, and be still."

MR. IMPORTANT WILL SPEAK AT THE CONVENTION

The famous *Mr. Important* arrived this morning in the big city to participate in the big business convention. Mr. Busy, the head of the convention's committee, said, "We are thrilled to have such an honorable guest at our convention. I'm sure many participants will benefit a lot from listening to Mr. Important's speech. He is one of the most respected speakers in the world and always has many serious topics to talk about."

BUSINESS & ECONOMY NEWS

A new company named Big Trade has reported huge economic growth in the past three months, and their stocks rose by hundreds of percentage points.

We asked the company's manager, Ms. Success, to share the secret of this unusual growth. "We work very hard and we constantly listen to the market's needs," she replied. We also asked for

say that I love rules, and I think that rules are most important to our society. The new rule must be studied carefully and applied immediately in order for our economy to grow at a steady pace."

But not everybody shares the enthusiasm. "I think that Big Trade is about to go down fast," said an anonymous source. "When you go up so quickly, you might fall down just as fast."

SPORTS NEWS

A new world record was set yesterday at the big athletic competition. Mr. Fast made a significant achievement when he ran the race at the highest speed ever recorded in human history. He won the gold medal and said, "This is a great moment for me, and I'm sure this is just

BIG DEAL NEWS

Special Edition   ***   Weekend News   ***   Volume 2867

A NEW RULE

In a special government meeting, the new rule was accepted and registered as federal law. Some of the participants objected to the change and said that this would be a big mistake. Ms. Law, who offered the new rule, was very happy with the decision and said, "A new era has now begun for many people who suffered until today. I thank all the participants of the meeting who understood the importance of this new rule a helped me to make it a reality."

Tomorrow will be the first meeting

of the co   hat was assigned to   k on   ng the new rule, and   th   weeks, all businesses acros   y will begin to make th   nges in order to imple- ment

is new rule,"

e growth

ke life a

       ss

     wners."

C   tinue rea

> "But I have an idea for a much better pose. See?" said Penny.
> "You can't pose like that in a newspaper. All things here must be serious," Mr. Important said.
> "That's the rule of Newspaper."

MR. IMPORTANT WILL SPEAK AT THE CONVENTION

The famous *Mr. Important* arrived this morning in the big city to participate in the big business convention. Mr. Busy, the head of the convention's committee, said, "We are thrilled to have such an honorable guest at our convention. I'm sure many participants will benefit a lot from listening to Mr. Important's speech. He is one of the most respected speakers in the world and always has many serious topics to talk about."

BUSINESS & ECONOMY NEWS

A new company named Big Trade has reported huge economic growth in the past three months, and their stocks rose by hundreds of percentage points.

We asked the company's manager, Ms. Success, to share the secret of this unusual growth. "We work very hard and we constantly listen to the market's needs," she replied. We also asked for her opinion about the new rule. "I

say that I love rules, and I think that rules are most important to our society. The new rule must be studied carefully and applied immediately in order for our economy to grow at a steady pace."

But not everybody shares the enthusiasm. "I think that Big Trade is about to go down fast," said an anonymous source. "When you go up so quickly

SPORTS NEWS

A new world record was set yesterday at the big athletic competition. Mr. Fast made a significant achievement when he ran the race at the highest speed ever record- ed in human hi

BIG DEAL NEWS

Special Edition *** Weekend News *** Volume 2867

A NEW RULE

In a special government meeting, the new rule was accepted and registered as federal law. Some of the participants objected to the change and said that this would be a big mistake. Ms. Law, who offered the new rule, was very happy with the decision and said, "A new era has now begun for many people who suffered until today. I thank all the participants of the meeting who understood the importance of this new rule and helped me to make it a reality."

Tomorrow will be the first meeting of the committee that was assigned to work on applying the new rule, and within three weeks, all businesses across the country will begin to make the necessary changes in order to implement the rule.

"I'm looking forward to this new rule," said Mr. Order. "It will create growth in the economy and will make life a lot easier, especially for small business owners."

Continue reading on p. 3

> Penny didn't like that rule at all, so she walked off the newspaper and onto a . . .

MR. IMPORTANT WILL SPEAK AT THE CONVENTION

The famous *Mr. Important* arr[...] in the big city to participate i[...] convention. Mr. Busy, the head o[...] committee, said, "We are thrilled [...] an honorable guest at our convention. [...] many participants will benefit a lot from [...] to Mr. Important's speech. He is one o[...] respected speakers in the world and a[...] as many serious topics to talk about."

BUSINESS & ECONOMY NEWS

A new company named Big Trade has reported huge economic growth in the past three months, and their stocks rose by hundreds of percentage points.

We asked the company's manager, Ms. Success, to share the secret of this unusual growth. "We work very hard and we constantly listen to the market's needs," she replied. We also asked for

say that I love rules, and I think that rules are most important to our society. The new rule must be studied carefully and applied immediately in order for our economy to grow at a steady pace."

But not everybody shares the enthusiasm. "I think that Big Trade is about to go down fast," said an anonymous

SPORTS NEWS

A new world record was set yesterday at the big athletic competition. Mr. Fast made a significant achievement when he ran the race at the hi[...]

MAP

"Who are you?" Penny asked a round, spiny creature she saw when she arrived.

"I'm Compass," said the creature.

"May I swim in your lake?" Penny asked.

"First you must go east and check if you're on the legend," said Compass.

Penny went to the legend and looked at all the drawings.

"I can't find myself on the legend," said Penny.

"Then I'm sorry, you'll have to leave," said Compass. "Only things that appear on the legend can be here. That's the rule of Map."

So Penny walked off the map and onto a piece of . . .

✿ MAP LEGEND ✿

Compass   Nature Park   Airport

River   Camping Site   Port

Road   Picnic Area   City

Railroad

Lookout Point   Village

Trail

Car Park   Train Station   Beach

GRAPH PAPER

"Who are you?" Penny asked a tall shape.

"I'm Rectangle," said the shape.

"I like the little squares on your paper," Penny said. "May I play hopscotch on them?"

"First you must fit inside a shape like me," answered Rectangle.

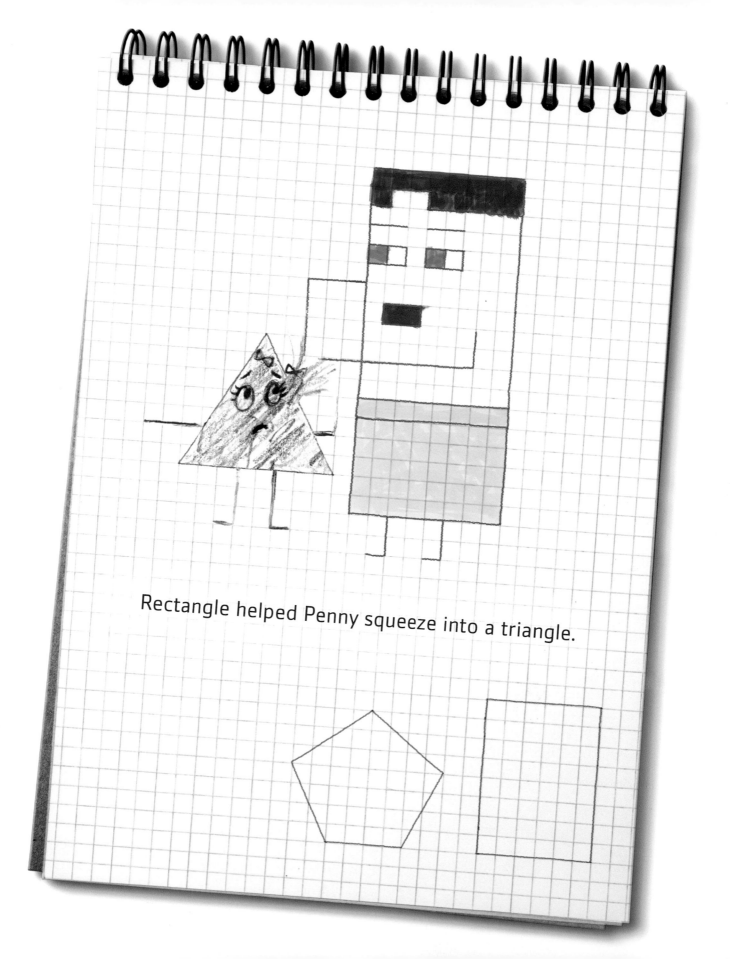

Rectangle helped Penny squeeze into a triangle.

Penny had to hold her breath.

Puff-puff-puff! When Penny let out her breath, her body puffed out of the triangle.

"Oh! What a mess!" said Rectangle. "I'm sorry, you'll have to leave. Only things that fit inside geometric shapes can be here. That's the rule of Graph Paper."

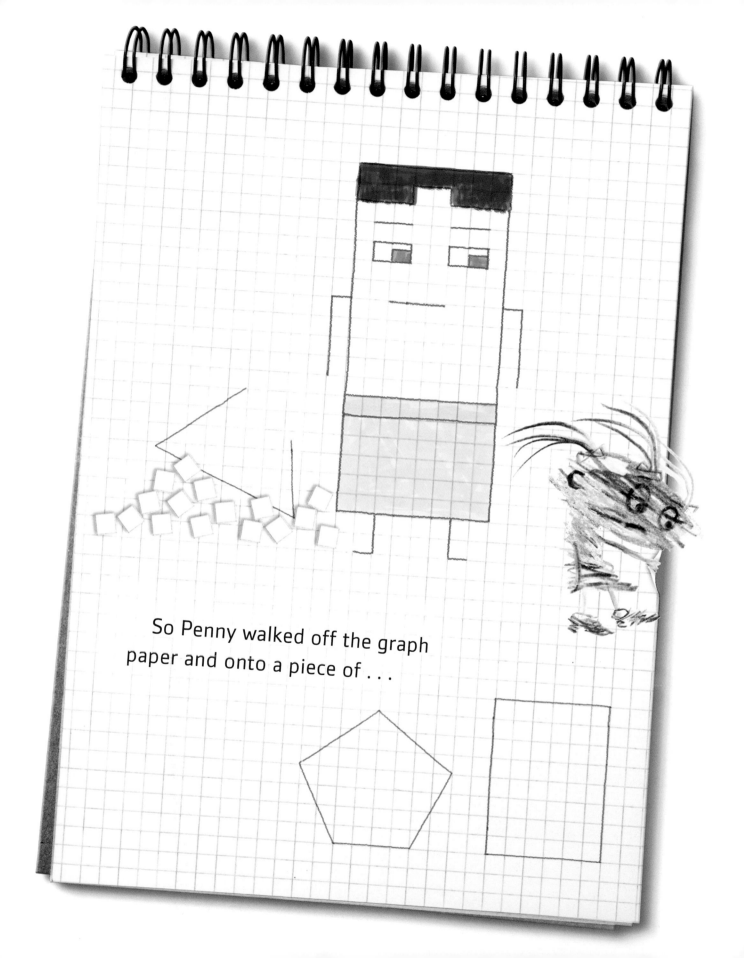

So Penny walked off the graph
paper and onto a piece of . . .

WRAPPING PAPER

Penny danced between colorful confetti flakes and balloons.

"Who are you?" she asked two children she saw walking along the paper.

"I'm the party-hat distributor," said the boy. "Want to wear one?"

"And I'm the present giver-outer," the girl said. "Would you like one?"

"Thank you," said Penny. "What a fun party!"
She continued to dance around until she heard somebody say:
"I'm the party-hat distributor. Want to wear one?"
"And I'm the present giver-outer. Would you like one?"
It was the same boy and girl. Penny was confused.
"Didn't you give me a hat and present already?" she asked.

She walked around and realized
that the two children were everywhere.
They kept giving her party hats and
presents, over and over.
 "Why do you keep asking the same
questions again and again?" wondered Penny.
 "We must repeat the same thing over and over,"
they told her. "That's the rule of Wrapping Paper."

Penny felt dizzy. She walked out
of the wrapping paper and into a . . .

COLORING BOOK

Penny walked up to the first animal she saw and asked, "Who are you?"

"I'm Mama Bear, and this is Baby Bear," the animal said. "Where is your outline?"

"My what?" asked Penny.

"There is no black line around your body," said Mama Bear.

"I never had one," said Penny.
"Can I please join you? I want to fly in a balloon!"
"First we need to add a black line around you," said Mama Bear.
"And then we need to remove your color," said Baby Bear.

When the bears were done, Penny felt empty.
"I miss my color," she cried.
"I'm sorry," said Mama Bear. "All things here must have an outline and no color. That's the rule of Coloring Book."

So Penny took her color back and pulled off her black outline.
She walked off the coloring book and onto a . . .

PLAIN PIECE OF PAPER

There's nothing here, Penny thought.

Maybe I can do something different about it.

So she got to work, and then sent an invitation to all her new friends.

"Welcome to my piece of paper," said Penny.

"Let's make our own rules!"

And they did.